"Pat, how long was I taking the Dirty Bubble challenge?" asked SpongeBob.

"About a week," answered Patrick calmly. "Maybe ten days."

"Ten days!" SpongeBob said, as the awful truth dawned on him.

He started rushing around his house searching for Gary and calling his name. He looked under his bed and in his closet. He looked in the toilet and the TV. He looked on the roof and under the sidewalk. He even looked inside the eggs in his refrigerator, but Gary was nowhere to be found.

"Patrick," he said, his eyes filling with tears. "I can't find Gary!"

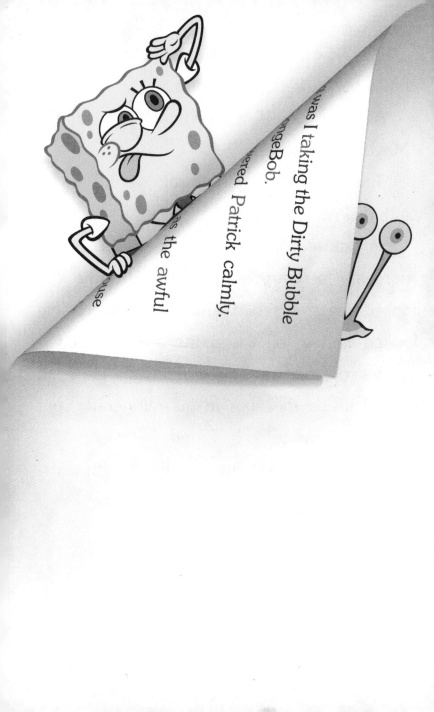

was I taking the Dirty Bubble

ongeBob.

ered Patrick calmly.

the awful

use

WHERE'S GARY?

Stephen Hillenburg

Based on the TV series *SpongeBob SquarePants*®
created by Stephen Hillenburg as seen on Nickelodeon®

SIMON SPOTLIGHT
An imprint of Simon & Schuster Children's Publishing Division
1230 Avenue of the Americas, New York, New York 10020

© 2007 Viacom International Inc. All rights reserved.
NICKELODEON, *SpongeBob SquarePants*, and all related titles, logos, and characters are registered trademarks of Viacom International Inc.
Created by Stephen Hillenburg.

Manufactured in the United States of America

First Edition
2 4 6 8 10 9 7 5 3 1

ISBN-13: 978-1-4169-4071-5
ISBN-10: 1-4169-4071-5

Library of Congress Catalog Card Number 2006925120

NICKELODEON

SPONGEBOB SQUAREPANTS

WHERE'S GARY?

adapted by **David Lewman**

illustrated by **Barry Goldberg**

based on a screenplay written by
Aaron Springer and **Paul Tibbitt**

Simon Spotlight/Nickelodeon

New York   London   Toronto   Sydney

chapter one

SpongeBob grunted. His legs shook. His arms ached. He was carrying home a big sack of food for his pet snail, Gary.

"Hey, SpongeBob!" called Patrick, who was standing by his rock house.

"Hey, Patrick," SpongeBob gasped.

"What are you doing?" asked Patrick cheerfully.

"Carrying this heavy bag of snail food for Gary," he wheezed.

Patrick grinned and leaned against his rock. "How *is* Gary?" he asked, ready for a nice, long talk.

SpongeBob felt as though his arms were about to drop off. "He's fine," he croaked. "Uh, Pat, could we talk about this some other time? This snail food is really heavy!" Perspiration was flying off SpongeBob's head.

"Oh, sure," said Patrick, patting his rock. "But there was something I wanted to tell you—something important." Patrick scratched his head, thinking hard. "Oh, I remember!"

But when Patrick looked, no one was there. "Uh, who was I talking to?" he asked.

SpongeBob dropped

the heavy bag of snail food on his front step and gasped for breath. Then he noticed a note on his front door!

He read the note as he walked inside. "Dear Sir or Ma'am: We are sorry we missed you. We will attempt to redeliver your package at our earliest convenience." Just as he finished reading, SpongeBob's doorbell rang. His package!

He opened the door and found a box wrapped in brown paper and string. SpongeBob was so excited that he dashed back inside with the box, forgetting all about Gary's bag of food.

"Let's see what we've got here!" said SpongeBob, tearing the package open. "My Official Mermaidman and Barnacleboy Paddleball Set! Whoo, yeah!" He pumped his fist, picked up the paddle, and whacked the red ball with it. The ball snapped back on its rubber string and smacked SpongeBob right in the head, knocking him to the ground.

Papers from inside the box fluttered down around SpongeBob. He peeled one off his face and read it. "Take the Dirty Bubble challenge: Hit the paddleball 29,998,559,671,349 times in a row."

SpongeBob fell to his knees and looked up. "Dirty Bubble," he cried, "wherever you float, I hereby accept your challenge!"

Determined to reach his goal, SpongeBob hit the rubber ball with the paddle. It snapped back and hit him in the face again. "Barnacles," he said. He tried several more times, but each time the ball struck him in the face. "Barnacles," he repeated again and again.

Meanwhile, Gary woke up from his nap feeling hungry. But when he looked in his food bowl, there was nothing but a fly, a couple of crumbs, and a spiderweb!

Gary watched the fly buzz away. He went back to SpongeBob, who was still trying to hit the ball without getting smacked in the face. "Meow!" Gary called, hungry.

"What was that?" asked SpongeBob, looking around. Shrugging, he started to go back to paddleballing, but then he heard an even louder meow.

"Oh! Gary!" he said, looking down at his snail. "That distracting sound came from you!" He turned back to his paddleball. "I'm sorry I can't play with you right now. Mermaidman needs me."

But just as SpongeBob was about to hit the red ball zooming toward his face, Gary meowed. Distracted, SpongeBob got smacked in the face—again.

"Gary, please!" he begged. "I'm trying to defeat the Dirty Bubble!" He showed his pet the red ball, but Gary just stuck himself to the paddle and meowed.

Annoyed, SpongeBob pulled Gary off his paddle. Then he went back to his goal: winning the Dirty Bubble challenge. A few moments later, SpongeBob got another smack in the face. Gary leaped right onto SpongeBob's face and suctioned himself there! "YAAAAAAAA! AAAAAA! AAAAAAAA!" SpongeBob cried while wrestling his pet snail from his face. "Gary, I HATE it when you do that! Now GET! And leave your master to his important affairs!"

Gary finally gave up. He slid back over to his bowl, tucked his head inside his shell, and sat silently. After a few days of feeling hungry and neglected, Gary decided that it was time to go and find a new home. He tied a polka-dot bandana onto a bamboo

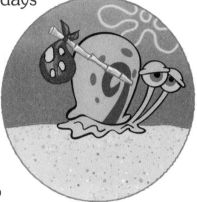

stick, packed his belongings inside, and left the pineapple he had called home for so long. He caught the first bus he saw, looking sadly out the window as it pulled away.

SNAILWAYS

chapter two

Patrick strolled from his rock house to SpongeBob's pineapple. "I haven't seen SpongeBob in a couple of days," he said to himself. "I'm sure he'll be glad to know I remembered what I wanted to tell him."

As he knocked on the door, Patrick stood right in front of the bag of snail food. "That's strange," he said to himself. "Usually I knock on the door with *this* hand." He shrugged and went inside.

"Hey, SpongeBob!" Patrick called. "Are you around? SpongeBob?" As Patrick made his way through the house, it seemed dark and scary to him. Things were knocked over and out of place. And he thought he could hear someone muttering "Barnacles" over and over.

Finally Patrick found SpongeBob curled up on the floor of his bedroom, trembling. Flies were buzzing all around him. "SpongeBob! What happened?" cried Patrick, rushing over. "This picture is crooked!" Patrick straightened the picture on the wall, then ran over to SpongeBob and turned him on his back.

SpongeBob was clutching the paddleball. "SpongeBob, snap out of it!" yelled Patrick. But SpongeBob still seemed very upset by

something. "What is it, buddy?" asked Patrick.
"You can tell me!"

"I took the Dirty Bubble challenge,"
SpongeBob admitted, holding up the paddleball.

"You what?!" shouted Patrick. Then he
broke into sobs and hung his head.

SpongeBob was puzzled. "Why are *you*
crying?" he asked.

Patrick stopped crying for a moment.

"Because many years ago, *I* took that challenge!" he answered.

"Really? What happened?" asked SpongeBob, sitting up.

"I won," said Patrick sadly. "But then I lost the trophy they sent me."

SpongeBob led Patrick into the kitchen. "Come on," he said. "Let's have some kelp cookies and fresh seahorse milk. That always cheers me up when I've lost something."

"Thanks, buddy," said Patrick.

After he handed Patrick a glass, SpongeBob walked back to his refrigerator to put away the milk. "Hey, Pat," he asked. "You ever feel like you're forgetting something? Something important?"

SpongeBob tripped right over Gary's food bowl. He picked it up and stared at it. "I think it

has something to do with this bowl . . . Gary's
food bowl." Suddenly he remembered! "That's
it! I gotta feed Gary!"

On his doorstep, SpongeBob found the bag

of snail food covered in dust. "That's a lot of dust for a couple of hours," he said, blowing away the dust and cobwebs.

Back in the kitchen, SpongeBob filled Gary's bowl. "Gary! Dinner! Come on, Gary! Soup's on! Gary?" But Gary didn't come.

"Pat, how long was I taking the Dirty Bubble challenge?" asked SpongeBob, his eye twitching nervously.

"About a week," answered Patrick calmly.

"A week?!" cried SpongeBob. "Are you sure?"

Patrick thought for a minute. Then he tried pouring the seahorse milk out of the glass. It slid slowly out, having gone bad and turned into a solid. Just to be sure, Patrick smelled the sour milk, popped it in his mouth, chewed it, and swallowed. Then he shuddered.

"Yeah, about a week," Patrick decided, based on how sour the milk tasted. "Maybe ten days."

"Ten days!" SpongeBob said, as the awful truth dawned on him.

He started rushing around his house searching for Gary and calling his name. He looked under his bed and in his closet. He looked in the toilet and behind the TV. He

looked on the roof and under the sidewalk. He
even looked inside the eggs in his refrigerator,
but Gary was nowhere to be found.

"Patrick," he said, his eyes filling with tears.
"I can't find Gary!"

chapter three

Gary was sliding along through an empty desert. He heard a terrible howling sound, which scared him until he realized it was just his empty stomach. He sneezed and kept going, all alone.

Back in his house, SpongeBob took a can out of the cupboard and showed it to Patrick. "These are Gary's favorite treats!" he said. "They're filled with eight types of organic sediment that bottom-feeders like Gary can't resist!"

"Eight?" asked Patrick, taking the can from SpongeBob and examining it.

SpongeBob nodded. "All you really have to do is shake the can. Gary comes running every time! Go on, try it!"

Patrick shook the can, but it didn't make a sound. SpongeBob was confused. "Let me see that!" he said. He shook the can, but it was silent.

"I don't understand," he said. "This is a brand new—"

"BURP!" belched Patrick. SpongeBob looked at Patrick suspiciously, then shook his belly. He could hear the snail treats rattling!

"I only tasted six types of sediment," Patrick complained.

SpongeBob and Patrick went outside to search for Gary. SpongeBob called his snail's name while Patrick shook his belly. *Rattle. Rattle. Rattle.*

With soapsuds on his head, Squidward

leaned out of his bathroom window. "What are those Neanderthals up to?" he grumbled. "Don't they know I'm busy spoiling myself?"

Squidward pulled his head back inside and resumed scrubbing his back with a brush. Suddenly SpongeBob and Patrick burst into his bathroom! "YAAAAAHH!" Squidward screamed.

But SpongeBob and Patrick just ignored

him. "You check over there," SpongeBob told Patrick. "I'll check in here." SpongeBob swished his hands around in Squidward's bathtub. "Find him yet, Pat?" he called.

"No," answered Patrick, yanking Squidward's sink off the wall, causing water to gush into the room. "But I'll keep looking!"

"But there's nowhere left to look!" cried SpongeBob as the room filled with water.

"There's one place we haven't checked!" announced Patrick dramatically.

SpongeBob and Patrick stood in front of SpongeBob's mailbox. It was jammed full of mail since SpongeBob hadn't checked it for days. "I doubt Gary could fit in there," SpongeBob protested.

"Can't hurt to look," said Patrick.

When SpongeBob pulled the door open,

mail came shooting out of the mailbox! The last thing to pop out was a rolled-up note.

"Look, Pat!" exclaimed SpongeBob.

"What is it?" asked Patrick.

SpongeBob unrolled the note and began to read the strange scratch-marks on the paper. "Dear SpongeBob," he read. "These past few years have been some of the best of my life, but I must move on. By now I have probably found a new owner who actually remembers to fill up my food bowl every now and again. Sincerely, Gary (at least until my new owner renames me)."

SpongeBob looked up from the note, stunned. "Dear Neptune," he murmured. "What have I done?"

Patrick looked stern. "What do you mean? You drove him away. It's right there in black and white!" He pointed at the note. "See? Right there . . . and there."

SpongeBob just stared out into the dark night. "Gary," he said miserably.

While SpongeBob mourned his missing snail, Gary used his last bit of energy to crawl toward a busy downtown area in hopes of finding food.

He stared through a window at a happy couple eating sandwiches until the man frowned at him and pulled down the shade. Gary was *very* hungry.

He slid into an alley and spotted a tray of old nachos! He hurried over to eat the cheesy chips, not even caring that there were flies buzzing around the leftovers.

Suddenly three tough alley snails hissed at Gary! He trembled with fear as they surrounded him. "Look who came to dinner!" growled the biggest, meanest-looking snail.

Gary shot out of the alley as fast as

his mucus could carry him. "Guess he didn't like nachos," said one of the snails. All three of them sighed, disappointed at losing their dinner guest.

Gary kept going as fast as he could, trying to get far away, but he bumped right into a pair of shoes! Shaking with fear, he looked up at a shadowy figure reaching down toward him.

"There you are," hissed a low, raspy voice.

chapter four

Gary hid in his shell, shaking. He peeked out and saw two sharp-clawed hands. They grabbed him, lifted, and . . .

Hugged him! "There you are, Miss Tuffsy!" said a kindly old woman with gray hair tied neatly in a bun. "Oh, Grandma finally found you. She was starting to get worried!"

She strolled out of the alley carrying Gary. "Now let's get you home, Miss Tuffsy, and get you something to eat," she said, smiling. Food sounded very good to Gary, no matter what name the sweet old lady called him.

In her house, Grandma set Gary on a big, comfy chair and fed him cookies. She even covered him with a warm electric blanket. "There you go, Miss Tuffsy," she said. "Grandma knows you like your Mister Heatie set to 'extra cozy' when you're home relaxing."

Gary didn't know who Grandma was (or Miss Tuffsy, for that matter), but he sure liked the way she was treating him! "Goodness!" cried Grandma. "You're almost out of cookies! Here, I'll go and get some more. Now don't you go running off again."

While Grandma was in the kitchen, Gary noticed a picture of her sitting in a chair surrounded by lots and lots of snails. She seemed to really love snails!

Soon she returned with lots more cookies. "There we go!" she said, smiling. "After this I'll make up some of those deviled eggs I promised."

While Gary munched happily on cookies, Grandma wandered over to her old record player. "How about a little music?" she asked. "Grandma's got a killer stereo system!"

She put on a record and started dancing around. Petting Gary, Grandma said, "You make Grandma feel so young!" She picked Gary up and whirled around with him. "Come on, Miss Tuffsy! Let's do the boogie-woogie!"

SNAP! Grandma felt a twinge in her back and quickly set Gary back down on the comfy chair. "Okay, that's enough of the boogie-woogie for now," she said.

While Gary was enjoying the comforts of Grandma's house, SpongeBob was still searching for his beloved snail. He wandered the streets of Bikini Bottom, calling, "GAAAARYYYYY!"

He was staring in the window of a hat store when he thought he saw his pet's reflection. "Gary!" he joyously exclaimed. But when he turned around, SpongeBob saw that it was just a picture of a snail on the side of a snail food delivery truck.

Sadly, he trudged on. He tried popping out of a chimney and loudly calling Gary's name into the night, but there was no answer. SpongeBob sobbed. Would he ever see his snail again?

chapter five

Gary sat on the couch under his electric blanket watching TV. Grandma had her arm around him and occasionally tossed popcorn in his mouth. "Grandma knows how much you love these late-night crime-drama programs," she said. "Don't you, Miss Tuffsy?"

Then Grandma noticed that it was seven thirty in the evening. "Oh, heavens!" she cried. "Look at the time! It's time for bed, Miss Tuffsy."

She got up and headed toward the bedroom.

Gary jumped off the couch to follow her, but when he pulled the electric blanket, the bundle of things he had taken from SpongeBob's house fell on the floor. There lay a picture of SpongeBob, smiling and waving. Gary meowed sadly.

But he was still hurt, and as he looked at the picture he began to imagine SpongeBob frowning and yelling, "Quiet, Gary! Can't you see I'm busy?!" So Gary stuck his tongue out at the picture and followed Grandma into his very own bedroom.

It was like

a baby's room, with stuffed animals and a crib. "Meow?" asked Gary, not sure he liked it.

But when Grandma tucked him into the crib, Gary felt very comfortable. "Oh!" said Grandma. "I almost forgot your good-night kiss!" She leaned in and kissed Gary.

From the doorway, Grandma whispered, "Sweet dreams, Miss Tuffsy!" before she clapped her hands and the lights snapped off.

The next morning at the Krusty Krab, SpongeBob plodded in looking terrible. His eyes were red with big circles under them, and his nose drooped. "SpongeBob!" yelled Mr. Krabs. "You're fifteen minutes late!"

"Sorry, Mr. Krabs," SpongeBob murmured. "I was out all night, looking for Gary. You see, he ran away, and now I—"

"SpongeBob, are you okay?" asked Mr. Krabs, sounding concerned. "You look kind of different." He leaned in for a closer look.

"Well, I'm not exactly what you'd call 'okay,' Mr. Krabs," answered SpongeBob. "You see, my—"

"Aha!" exclaimed Mr. Krabs, snapping his claw. "You just forgot to put your hat on!" He slapped a Krusty Krab hat on SpongeBob's head and walked away, saying, "Knew I'd figure it out!"

In the kitchen, SpongeBob tried frying up some delicious Krabby Patties, but his tears kept running down his nose and dripping on the patties. "Gary!" he squeaked.

A customer confronted Squidward. "Yeah, I'd like a refund for this Krabby Patty," she complained.

Mr. Krabs came running. "Refund?! What's wrong with it?"

"Oh, nothing really," the customer answered sarcastically, "except that it's covered in tears!"

She lifted the top bun and Mr. Krabs saw tears glistening on the surface of the patty. "What the . . . ?" he muttered.

Mr. Krabs went in the kitchen and found SpongeBob crying. "Why don't you tell me what's wrong?"

"Well, you see—," SpongeBob began.

"Listen to me, boy," Mr. Krabs interrupted. "Any problem you have can be solved with a little hard work."

Then he held up SpongeBob's spatula, hoping he'd get back to work.

SpongeBob snapped out of his depression. "You're right, Mr. Krabs!"

Mr. Krabs smiled and said, "That's my boy!"

"If I'm going to find Gary, I'm going to need to work harder at it!" Then SpongeBob ran out of the kitchen, leaving Mr. Krabs speechless.

chapter six

Patrick was lying on the warm sand, snoring loudly. Drool dribbled out of the corner of his mouth. Suddenly a pile of paper, pencils, tape, glue, and paste fell on him, waking him up!

"It's the end of the world!" he cried. "Office products falling from the sky!" Then he looked up. SpongeBob was standing over him with his arms stretched out.

"No, Patrick!" he said. "We're gonna use this

stuff to help us find Gary!"

Patrick sat up, puzzled. "But I thought you drove him away with your neglect and indifference."

SpongeBob sighed, then looked determined.

"Patrick, now is not the time for talking. We've got work to do!"

At Grandma's house, Gary was enjoying a breakfast of fresh-squeezed orange juice and pancakes shaped like gingerbread men. Grandma even fed Gary by hand, carefully guiding each bite into his wide-open mouth.

After breakfast, they got into Grandma's car and drove to a store called Martha's Craft Zone. "Set phasers on 'fun,' Miss Tuffsy," said Grandma with a smile.

Just moments after Grandma and Gary went into the store, SpongeBob and Patrick arrived loaded down with posters. "Here's a good spot!" SpongeBob said, rolling one of the posters open, ready to paste it on the front door.

He read his poster out loud to make sure it was just right. "Gary, I am sorry. Please come home. Love, SpongeBob." He thought that said it all.

"Quick, Patrick, hand me the tape!" he said. But Patrick was studying another sign on the front door. "Hey, they're having a sale on

scented pinecones!" Patrick exclaimed.

"Patrick, this is no time for that!" SpongeBob protested. But he was too late. Patrick rushed inside the store, chanting, "Pinecones, pinecones, pinecones!"

Grandma was admiring some pipe cleaners when Patrick hurried up to her. "Old lady, quick!" he blurted. "I'm looking for the scented pinecones! It's an emergency!"

But Grandma told him she'd already picked up all they had. She showed Patrick her basket full of pinecones, and he leaned in to smell them. "Once again, you and I are kept apart, oh sweet-scented pinecones," he said sadly.

On his way out, he spotted Gary by her side. "Hey, Gary," he called out. Gary blinked.

Outside, SpongeBob had just finished covering the front of the store with missing-

snail posters. "There!" he said, satisfied with his work.

Then Patrick opened the front door, ripping through several posters. "Oops," he said, trying to somehow put the torn posters back together.

SpongeBob handed Patrick a stack of flyers. "Come on, Pat! Just take these flyers and hand them out!" They walked away from the store.

Seconds later, Grandma led Gary out balancing a basket of scented pinecones on his shell. He didn't see SpongeBob, and SpongeBob didn't see him.

chapter seven

After a full day of shopping, with lots of treats and snacks, Grandma and Gary walked in the front door. "Grandma will get a lovely meatloaf in the oven for you," she said. Gary wasn't feeling hungry. In fact, he already felt stuffed.

He slid onto the messy newspapers in the corner and meowed. "Oh, Miss Tuffsy!" Grandma said. "Do you have to go potty?" She dropped a big pile of papers in front of Gary.

"Why don't you use this stack of flyers given to me today by a chubby little boy?" While Grandma returned to her kitchen, Gary looked at the flyers. They were SpongeBob's flyers! SpongeBob was sorry! And he wanted Gary to come home!

Gary started to slide toward the door, but then he heard a sharp whistle. "You stay right there," Grandma warned. "The meatloaf is almost done."

Gary sighed heavily. The last thing he wanted was meatloaf. Grandma had been stuffing him with food ever since he arrived! Seeing Patrick at the craft store made Gary realize how much he missed SpongeBob. And now that Gary knew SpongeBob missed him, too, and wanted him to come home, Gary was ready to go!

So he made his way to what he thought was the front door and turned the handle. When the door opened, dozens of empty snail shells came tumbling out! Most of them had cracks and holes in them. Had all of Grandma's snails been forced to eat until they burst out of their shells? What happened to all of these snails?

Grandma stepped into the hallway, looking a little less innocent than she had before. "The meatloaf's not quite ready yet, but Grandma knows how hungry you are, Miss Tuffsy, so she whipped up a quick batch of cookies."

Lying on the pile of empty shells, Gary looked down at his stomach. He had grown so fat that he burst his belt buckle! Then he cracked a hole in his shell! He imagined all the snails in the picture on the wall screaming, "RUN!"

As fast as he could, Gary escaped through the pet flap in the front door, dodging the cookies Grandma threw at him as he went. Out on the sidewalk, she chased after Gary.

"You don't want cookies? Don't fret! I made a batch of deviled eggs, too!" Grandma tossed food at Gary as he hurried to get away.

He slipped into a dark alley, but Grandma was still coming. "Don't worry, Miss Tuffsy!" she called. "Grandma will find you!" Gary hid behind a trash can.

One of the tough-looking alley snails he'd run into before recognized Gary. "Hey," he said. "You're that guy who doesn't like nachos!"

Grandma was getting closer. "Miss Tuffsy, I know you're back there!" she said. "I can hear your stomach growling."

Gary got an idea. He pushed the alley snail onto the sidewalk where Grandma could see him. "Hey!" the tough snail said, annoyed at being shoved.

"Oh, there you are, Miss Tuffsy!" exclaimed Grandma.

"Who?" asked the snail.

"You must be starving," Grandma said, scooping him up into her arms and walking away.

Gary sighed with relief.

chapter eight

Sitting on his couch with his fists clenched, SpongeBob was so sad he felt like sobbing, but he couldn't. Patrick was trying to comfort him. "Just let it out, buddy," he said. "That's right."

"I can't cry anymore, Patrick. When Gary left, he took all of my tears with him."

When he heard the name "Gary," Patrick sat up and widened his eyes. "Did you just say 'Gary'?"

SpongeBob nodded sadly. "SpongeBob!" Patrick said, excited. "I just remembered! Earlier today, at the craft store, I saw . . . these huge hunks of balsa wood! They were AWESOME!"

SpongeBob's eyes filled with tears. "Gary LOVED balsa wood!" he wailed, running out of the house.

"I gotta try to forget Gary," SpongeBob said to himself as he went for a walk, passing dozens and dozens of his own missing-snail flyers that he'd posted. "For some reason, I can't get him out of my mind."

He stared up at a big billboard with Gary's picture and huge letters spelling out "Have You Seen Me?"

"I blew it," he moaned. "I really blew it. I took you for granted, Gary. I'm sorry. Don't just stare at me! Say something!"

SpongeBob shrugged and looked down at the ground. "I'm talking to a billboard."

Behind him, there was a quiet meow.

"Now I'm hearing things!" he said. "If only I could see you one more time, so I could tell you how much I love you. If only I could hear you meow one last time."

Gary climbed up onto SpongeBob's head and meowed again.

"Yeah, like that," said SpongeBob.

Laying his eyeballs against SpongeBob's forehead, Gary purred loudly.

"Gary, your purring is making it hard to forget you," said SpongeBob. Suddenly he realized who he was talking to! "GARY!" he yelled, thrilled.

SpongeBob hugged Gary. "Oh, Gary! So, did you hear any of that, or do I have to repeat myself?"

"Meow," said Gary.

"Okay, good," SpongeBob said. "I promise,

Gary, things are going to be different between you and me. You'll see, pal! Now let's go home and get you something to eat. You must be starving!"

Gary just meowed.